CALIB AND QUARAN-TEEN

Written by Natori Blue

Illustrated by Victor Tavares

Life's been pretty good
As far as I can tell
Some bumps, some changes here and there
But I have managed well

My family, my school
My friendships all intact,
We had a way of doing things,
we had it all down pat

2

Before this guy named Quaran-Teen
I lived quite normally
Then he snatched normal from my hands
Just listen, you will see…

He sent toilet paper pirates
Into every grocery store
And the plundering continued
Until there was no more

So when at home and suddenly
I feel the urge to go
I have to close my eyes and pray
There's some left on the roll

When Quaran-Teen arrived
He sent all the barbers home
And we were forced to manage
Growing crowns all on our own

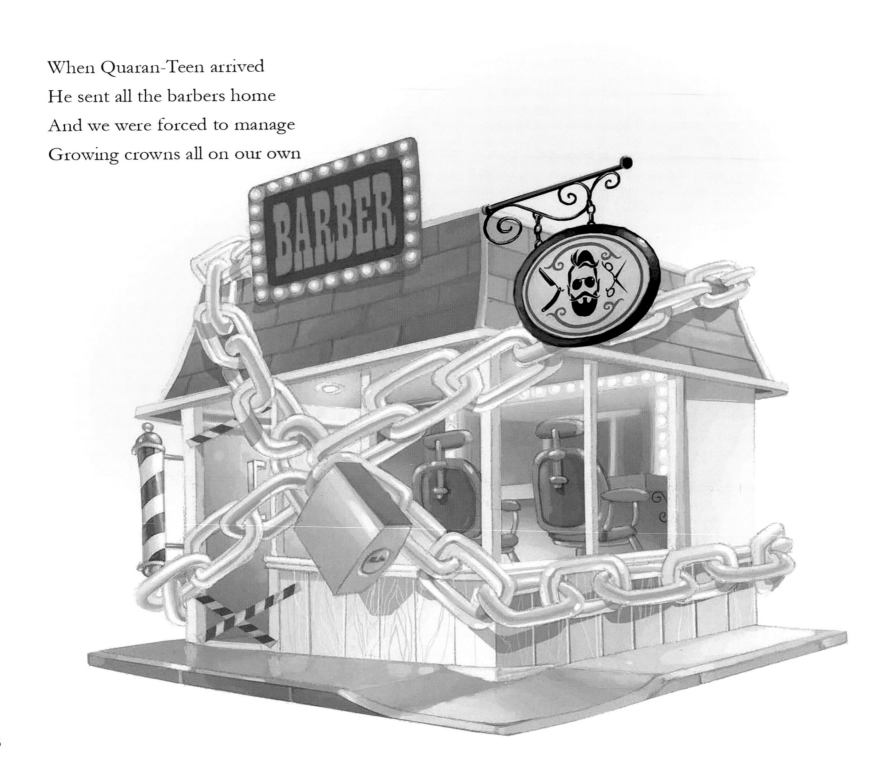

I used to get my hair cut low
With fancy art designs
But now it's hard to tell
My sister Kya's hair from mine

Quaran-Teen did not stop there
For he was on a roll
Dishing out the birthday blues
To victims young and old

What used to be a lively bash
With games and finger foods
Became a slew of weird phone calls:
Aunt Kat, Pop Sam and Jude

He then convinced the teachers,
"Work from your cozy homes!"
But classwork seems much harder
When you're going it alone

The letters get all jumbly
The numbers run amuck
Instructions so confusing that
I want to pass the buck

10

And what teen did to fashion
Well, he should be ashamed
He hid all the presentables
The people had obtained

Mismatches in the morning
Old T-shirts noon and night
To top it off, a plain white mask
To seal our styleless plight

11

And as if Quaran-Teen
Had not been cruel enough
When Grandpa Mike got sick
He made our "visit" really rough

Changed hospital policy
From two guests per room, to none
To see Gramps helpless on that screen
Just tortured this grandson

And when completely certain
That I'd surely lost my wits
I felt a gentle nudge and heard
"Son, I will handle this."

Little did I know
Or to what extent
Quaran-Teen had met his match
And she would not relent

Early in the morning
Before we could see light
The operation, it commenced
Super Mom took flight

She did a little shopping
With the pirates still asleep
A tissue tower
Just enough to get us through the week

Super Mom agreed with me
Could stand my mane no more
She draped her cape around me,
As I criss-crossed on the floor

16

The clippers started buzzing
When it all came to an end
There was no fancy art
But neither was I Kya's twin

Determined more than ever
To make the best of things
"New party plans to make," Mom said.
"Take this, Quaran-Teen!"

18

Covering my front yard porch
There were gifts galore,
And a party caravan:
I couldn't have asked for more

19

Super Mom was in her zone
Her chair pulled next to mine
Perused the task, with one inhale
Told me we would be fine

We rolled our eyes, we kicked and cried
Everything it took
And when at last we hit submit
We sighed and turned and shook

On to the pressing issue
Of everyday attire
The mirror could not even offer
One piece to admire

But Super Mom was on the case
Paired with the internet
Homemade masks and brand new pj's
Formed the perfect sets

21

EMERGENCY

Just one last task remaining
To offset Quaran-Teen
And yep, you guessed it, she was there
Already on the scene

But not for the reason
That I thought she was
She pulled me to a bench nearby
She pursed her lips and shrugged

22

Mom asked if I remembered
How we would gather 'round
While Grandpa Mike would tell us
War stories, 'loud and proud'

I nodded to confirm
As she explained to me
This was likely the last battle
Grandpa Mike would see

The family grew around us
The closest we could get
We watched our worst nightmare unfold
A heart-wrenching event

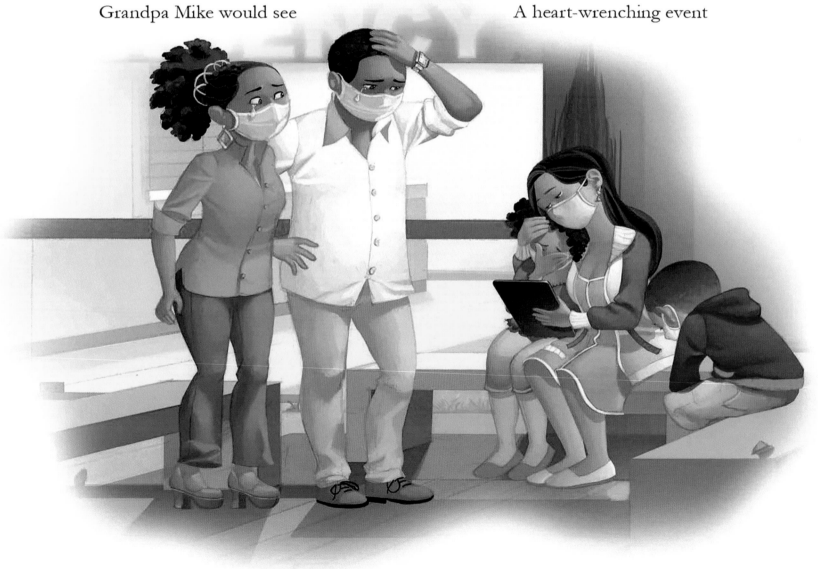

Now, I was crazy furious
Man, let this be a dream
Still turning my life upside down
Is that kid Quaran-Teen!

"Calm down now," my uncle said
"Things are as they should be
Placing blame won't stop the pain
Your heart needs this journey"

"Now, Quaran-Teen is challenging
But he is no bad guy
He may have rubbed us the wrong way
But hear the reason why

27

A little foe we could not see
Became a mighty threat
And Quaran-Teen chose to respond
Quite brave I must admit

You see he means to do no harm
His intentions are good
His unique style, intrusive ways
Are just misunderstood"

I paused a while to take this in
Discovered I agreed
A new perspective I had found
I'd misjudged Quaran-Teen

He did steal ordinary
But I was unaware
That emptying the barber shops
Was bigger than my hair

So I'll give him a break
Besides, he won't be here forever
During his stay, I'll try my best
To support his endeavours

Still can't quite wrap my head around
The changes that I see
But I'll keep cleverly adapting
Finding "normal" by degrees

31

This book is dedicated to the fearless medical professionals, first responders and all essential employees. —The true super heroes.